Also available:

The Not-so-Little Princess:

What's My Name?
Best Friends!
Spooky Night!

The Not-so-Little Princess

COLOUR READER

Where's Gilbert?

Wendy Finney
Tony Ross

ANDERSEN PRESS

This edition published in 2017 by
Andersen Press Limited
20 Vauxhall Bridge Road
London SW1V 2SA
www.andersenpress.co.uk

First published in 2015 by
Andersen Press Limited

1 3 5 7 9 10 8 6 4 2

British Library Cataloguing in Publication Data available.

ISBN: 978 1 78344 523 3

Printed and bound in Malaysia by
Tien Wah Press

Contents

Chapter 1

One bright summer's day, everyone
in the castle was busy doing the
things that you would expect them
to be doing. The King was in the
counting house counting out his
money. The Queen was in the
parlour eating bread and honey.
However, the maid had got someone
else to do the laundry as it was her
day off!

The Not-so-Little Princess Rosie was sitting in the sunshine under the big rose bush. She was thinking up stories and telling them out loud to Gilbert, her teddy, who was looking into her eyes and listening very carefully.

She had just got to the part in her story where Prince Billy had fallen down a big hole, landed upside down in a puddle of mud and been rescued by the fire brigade, when she saw her friend Ollie coming through the vegetable garden. He was doing his usual funny walk. Grabbing her teddy, Rosie jumped to her feet and waved at him.

She was just about to go and meet
him, when she looked down at the
bear in her arms.

"I can't let him see me with a
teddy!" she said to herself. "He'll
think I'm a baby."

Feeling very silly, she stuffed poor
Gilbert into the bush behind her and
hoped Ollie hadn't seen . . .

"What's THAT?!" said Ollie
jumping from one foot to the other.
He pointed to the bush where
Gilbert was hanging by one arm.

"What's WHAT?!" asked Rosie.

She had to think fast or Ollie would find out that she still played with her bear.

"THAT!" he said and dived into the rose bush before she could stop him.

He pulled out Gilbert and smiled.

"Ah, poor old ted," he said. "How could you dump him in a bush, old bean – that's just mean! I expect he has been a good friend to you . . ."

Rosie pretended she didn't care. Snatching Gilbert out of Ollie's hands, she stuffed him back in the bush.

"Oh well, he isn't mine!" said Rosie, going pink in the face. "He belongs to my baby brother, Prince Billy . . . er . . . he lost a leg so I was stitching him up . . . erm . . . not my brother of course, HE didn't lose a leg . . . the teddy . . . he lost a leg and um . . ."

What a fibber, thought Gilbert.
How could she say all that about me?
There is nothing wrong with my legs.
And he went into a sulk.

Ollie just looked at Rosie with his
jolly smile spreading over his face.
Rosie wasn't sure if he believed her
fib at all.

Chapter 2

Rosie and Ollie ran off into the sunshine to play some games. They left Gilbert all alone dangling in the bush and feeling sorry for himself.

Ladybirds and beetles crawled over him. A caterpillar walked up his leg and tummy then over his nose and into his ear.

This is too much for a royal teddy to put up with. I hope she comes back to collect me soon, he thought.

But hours and hours went by and soon darkness crept up over the gardens. The night creatures came out and began making their strange noises.

Gilbert had a touch of the colly wobbles, which as your Granny would know, means he was a bit scared.

Back at the castle, Ollie had gone home and it was Rosie's bedtime.

"Have you seen Gilbert?" she said to her maid.

"Silly girl!" exclaimed Maidy. "Can't you remember where you left him?"

But Rosie was too tired to think and after being tucked firmly in her comfy bed she soon fell asleep . . .

She awoke suddenly in the darkest hour of the night and remembered where she had left her old teddy.

I must go and get him now, he will be scared all alone!

She climbed out of bed and tiptoed over to her bedroom door which always creaked loudly when it was opened.

The long corridor outside was dark. She could see hardly anything but she found her way by the moonlight.

She had a scary feeling in her tummy, but being brave, she carried on until she came to the large painting of Great-grand Uncle Montgomery on the wall above the main staircase.

The moon lit up his fearsome eyes and it seemed as if he were looking straight at her . . .

"Eeek!" She squealed in fright and scurried back along the corridor into her bedroom and her warm bed . . .

It's only a painting, she kept telling herself, but still . . . She turned over, stuck her thumb firmly in her mouth and went back to sleep.

Gilbert would have to wait until tomorrow . . .

Chapter 3

The next morning Gilbert was still hanging in the rose bush.

"What's this?" said a voice.

Gilbert was pulled out of the bush and into the bright sunshine by a large boy holding an axe.

It was Jack, the woodcutter's son, who sometimes came to help in the castle gardens.

"It's some old teddy – looks as if it has been here for years," he said to himself.

I am not an old teddy! I am a royal teddy – and I've only been here for a night, thought Gilbert. He tried to kick the boy, but of course, nothing happened.

Jack just stuffed Gilbert into his pocket and forgot about him for the rest of the day.

That afternoon Jack was pulling out some reeds from the river bank. He leaned too far over and *SPLASH!* Gilbert slipped out of his pocket and into the stream.

"I have turned into a FISH!"
gurgled Gilbert. "This is fun!"
Flapping his arms and legs, he was
whisked away by the fast flowing
water, down over the meadow,
out of the castle grounds and into
the green and sunny countryside
beyond.

Just as he was about to go under
a bridge, a dustbin lorry full of bin
men came along the road. One
of the men saw Gilbert so they
stopped. The bin man fished Gilbert
out of the water.

"What you got there, Fred?"
called the driver.

"An old teddy bear – I'm going to add him to the collection."

He squeezed the water out of Gilbert and stuck him on the front of the lorry along with the other interesting bits and pieces found by the bin men: old rag dolls, plastic flowers and broken toys.

"You're a smart-looking bear –
what are you doing here with us?"
said a one-eyed doll.

"I don't know," said Gilbert,
with his nose in the air. "I belong
to Rosie, the princess of all the
land . . . I am her favourite toy."

"Yeah! A likely story! I bet Princess Rosie just got fed up with you and threw you away! Who do you think you are, Mr High-and-Mighty! Fluffybum! GERROFF!" and with that, the one-eyed doll pushed Gilbert so hard he fell off the dustcart and on to the dusty road. He rolled around in the dirt as the cart roared off on its way.

Gilbert lay by the side of the road, feeling sorry for himself.

That wasn't a nice thing to happen. What a horrid dolly! he thought. *Maybe Rosie* doesn't *care about me – after all she did try to hide me in the rose bush.* Gilbert stared down at his dusty toes, thinking deeply. But being a happy sort of bear, he cheered himself up by thinking nice thoughts.

Luckily for Gilbert, Rosie *was* thinking about him. She had got up that morning and gone straight out to find him, but of course, when she went to look for him in the rose bush, he wasn't there.

She'd asked the King and Queen if they had seen her teddy bear. And she asked everyone in the castle to help her look for him.

By lunchtime they had all been looking for dear old Gilbert for hours but he couldn't be found . . . oh dear.

Chapter 4

Gilbert was still lying by the road when along came a gang of rowdy schoolboys on their way to play football. Chatting noisily, they stopped when they saw the old teddy.

One boy, Davey, picked Gilbert up and tucked him under his arm.

When they got to the football field, Big Lenny grabbed Gilbert from Davey. He gave Gilbert an almighty kick as if he were a football.

Poor Gilbert went up, up, up into the air – higher than the rooftops then back again.

He landed straight into the gaping jaws of a scruffy little black-and-white dog that woofed and leaped around in excitement. He ran off across the playing field carrying Gilbert with him.

"Oi! I found him," shouted Davey, but it was too late. The dog had gone and the teddy had gone with him.

The dog ran through the town with Gilbert held tightly in his jaws. He was pleased with his prize and he was going to take him home.

A little girl called Annie was playing with her dolls on the doorstep when her dog came in through the back gate.

He ran straight up to Annie and pushed the teddy into her hands.

"Wow . . . what have you found, Wally?" she said, giving her pet a quick rub on his hairy head.

"Woof!" Wally looked very pleased with himself and gave Gilbert a wet sloppy lick all over.

YUCK! That is horrible and slimy! thought Gilbert. *Maidy washes me at least once a year and that is bad enough!*

"Come on," Annie said to Gilbert. "I am going to put you in my bag and take you out with us this afternoon. Mum said we are going somewhere special."

Down in the gardens by the Town
Hall, *The Interesting Antiques TV
Show* had come to town. The show
was very popular with people who
liked to collect old things. Annie's
mum, Mrs Witherinshaw, had
bought tickets to go to it.

The clever presenter Tom Whatalot was about to go in front of the TV cameras and talk about a rather battered old bear that Mrs Witherinshaw had brought along.

As he was having his nose powdered by the make-up girls, and chatting to Mrs Witherinshaw, Annie had an idea . . .

"I will put my new teddy on the table too so he can make friends with that manky old bear," she said to herself.

Annie opened her bag and dumped Gilbert down on the table right next to the old bear.

When Tom Whatalot turned back, he was shocked. Ignoring the old teddy, he stared hard at Gilbert.

"Mrs Witherinshaw!" he said, picking Gilbert up. "In all my years on this show, I have never seen such a rare and valuable teddy – where did you get him?" He turned Gilbert upside down to look at his label.

How rude! thought Gilbert. *It's not nice to turn teddies upside down without asking them first!*

Chapter 5

Mrs Witherinshaw was speechless, probably for the first time in her life. "I . . . I . . . I . . ." she spluttered.

"Well," said Tom Whatalot, "this teddy is very rare indeed and I would say . . . worth at least three thousand p-p-p . . ."

Just then, there was a flurry of brown feathers about the table and

a huge eagle snatched Gilbert out of
Tom Whatalot's hands and carried
him off high into the air.

UP ... UP ... UP and AWAY!
thought Gilbert. *This is thrilling –*
I have never had so much excitement
in the whole of my teddy life!

"WHEEEEEEEEEEEEEEE!!!!!" he cried in delight as he flew upwards carried by the bird. "Now I am a bird and I can fly!" He tried to flap his arms like wings.

The big brown eagle took a good look at this strange object he was carrying in his talons. *You aren't a bird and you can't fly either,* he thought. *You certainly won't make a good supper for my chicks – so here goes!* With that, he let go of the little teddy.

Gilbert looked at his flapping arms and a terrible realisation came over him – he didn't have wings after all!

He started to drop like a stone!

Meanwhile, Rosie was still looking for Gilbert. When she last saw him, she hadn't been very nice to him.

"Perhaps that will teach you a lesson to look after your things," nagged Maidy, and she toddled off to get on with making some jam tarts to try to cheer Rosie up.

Ollie came round again. He saw
that Rosie was very sad.

"You shouldn't be ashamed of
being fond of an old teddy," he said.
"Let me show you what I love."
He pulled out a dirty pink floppy
toy from his back pocket.

"May I introduce you to Midge," he said, waving it under Rosie's nose. "This is what is left of my old toy rabbit." One eye was hanging on a piece of thread and one ear was completely missing but Ollie gazed at him lovingly. "I will never part with him." He carefully put Midge back in his pocket.

"You're right, I should never have been embarrassed about still loving Gilbert,' said Rosie.

Then she had an idea. "I know! Let's make 'Lost Bear' posters to put up around the castle."

"That's a good idea," said Ollie.

Rosie got out some paper and pens. She drew pictures of Gilbert and Ollie did the writing.

Then they went and stuck them up everywhere around the castle.

Chapter 6

Rosie and Ollie spent all day putting up posters and asking everyone they met if they had seen Gilbert.

"Goodness knows where he is!" Rosie said to Ollie. They slumped down by the pond to think about what else they could do to find him.

"He may be in someone else's toy box by now, being looked after by some other little girl! She may not care for him properly. In fact, I may never see him again!"

Ollie looked closely at his friend's face.

Her mouth had turned down at the corners and her bottom lip was quivering.

Rosie was going to burst into tears.

High in the sky above, the big bird had just decided it didn't want this hairy brown thing it had snatched and let Gilbert go.

Gilbert came rushing down . . .

passing clouds and trees . . .

. . . and landed with a *plonk!*

. . . right in Rosie's lap!

She couldn't believe her eyes!

Ollie couldn't believe his eyes either – he took off his glasses and cleaned them just to make sure he wasn't seeing things.

"Oh Gilbert! I thought I had lost you forever!" Rosie squashed Gilbert in the biggest hug she had ever given him.

You will never guess where I have been and what I have done! thought Gilbert. *I swam like a fish and flew like a bird and I am worth three thousand p-p-p . . .*

Rosie gave Gilbert another huge squeeze.

"I don't care where you have been – I will never be horrid to you again. I missed you SO much! I am just SO glad you are home," she said.

AND SO YOU SHOULD BE! thought Gilbert as loudly as he could, and he gave himself an extra squeeze, just for luck.

And so Rosie, Ollie and Gilbert
went off to the kitchen to eat the
jam tarts Maidy had baked.

What a relief it was to get Gilbert
back!

And as for Mrs Witherinshaw's old teddy, he was taken home, washed and given the name "Harry", and now has pride of place in Annie's toy box!

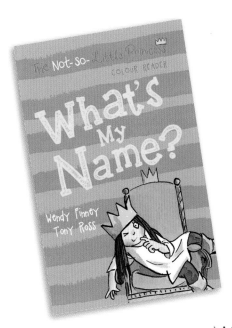

The Little Princess

is not so little any more!

Now that she's growing up, people can't keep calling her the LITTLE Princess. But her real name is horrible and no one dares tell her what it is!

What will the Not-so-Little Princess do when she finds out?

The Little Princess
has got a brand new friend!

The Princess's new friend
Ollie is different in every way
- from his funny old-fashioned
voice to his odd clothes.

And when they go exploring,
there's a BIG surprise in store
for them ...